A NOTE TO PARENTS

When your children are ready to "step into reading," giving them the right books—and lots of them—is as crucial as giving them the right food to eat. **Step into Reading Books** present exciting stories and information reinforced with lively, colorful illustrations that make learning to read fun, satisfying, and worthwhile. They are priced so that acquiring an entire library of them is affordable. And they are beginning readers with an important difference—they're written on four levels.

Step 1 Books, with their very large type and extremely simple vocabulary, have been created for the very youngest readers. **Step 2 Books** are both longer and slightly more difficult. **Step 3 Books,** written to mid-second-grade reading levels, are for the child who has acquired even greater reading skills. **Step 4 Books** offer exciting nonfiction for the increasingly proficient reader.

Children develop at different ages. **Step into Reading Books,** with their four levels of reading, are designed to help children become good—and interested—readers *faster*. The grade levels assigned to the four steps—preschool through grade 1 for Step 1, grades 1 through 3 for Step 2, grades 2 and 3 for Step 3, and grades 2 through 4 for Step 4—are intended only as guides. Some children move through all four steps very rapidly; others climb the steps over a period of several years. These books will help your child "step into reading" in style!

FOR

JOSH TOBIN

Library of Congress Cataloging–in–Publication Data
Hayes, Geoffrey. The curse of the Cobweb Queen / by Geoffrey Hayes. p. cm. — (Step into reading. A Step 3 book)
SUMMARY: Cousin Olivia proves to be very helpful when Otto and Uncle Tooth, a famous detective, attempt to retrieve a stolen black pearl from a wicked witch.
ISBN 0-679-83878-3 (trade)—0-679-93878-8 (lib. bdg.)
[1. Alligators–Fiction. 2. Witches–Fiction. 3. Mystery and detective stories.] I. Title II. Series: Step into reading. Step 3 book   PZ7.H31455Cu   1994
[E]—dc20   92-37272

Manufactured in the United States of America   10

STEP INTO READING is a trademark of Random House, Inc.
New York, Toronto, London, Sydney, Auckland

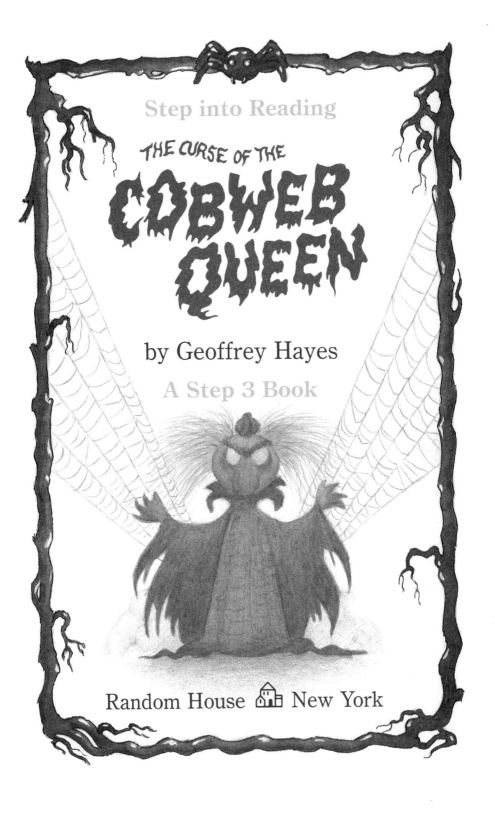

Step into Reading

THE CURSE OF THE

COBWEB QUEEN

by Geoffrey Hayes

A Step 3 Book

Random House 🏠 New York

ONE

Otto and Auntie Hick were waiting at the train station. Otto's cousin Olivia was coming for a visit. But Otto was more interested in playing marbles.

"Get up this minute!" Auntie Hick scolded. "Your new suit will get dirty."

Otto hated the new suit Auntie Hick had made for him.

"All this fuss for a *girl*!" he thought.

The train pulled into the station, and the passengers got off. Otto and Auntie Hick did not see Olivia anywhere.

"Maybe she decided to stay home," said Otto.

Auntie Hick asked Mr. Willie, the engineer, if he had seen her.

Before Mr. Willie could answer, Otto
cried, "There she is!"

They saw Olivia running from the
back of the train.

They called, but she did not hear
them.

"I'll get her," said Otto.

At first Otto lost sight of Olivia in the crowd. Then he caught sight of her again as she ran into an alley.

"Where on earth are you going?" he asked when he caught up with her.

"Quiet!" she whispered. "I'm following an old lady who was on the train."

"Why?" Otto whispered back.

"I don't trust her," Olivia replied. "She said she was feeling dizzy. But as soon as the train stopped, she climbed out a window so fast she forgot her purse."

Olivia held up a small black bag.

Otto said, "Are you trying to be a detective or something?"

"Maybe," said Olivia. "Are *you*?"

Before Otto could answer, they came to the end of the alley. But they did not find an old lady—only a sailor mending fishnets.

"She gave us the slip," said Olivia as they headed back to the station. "I'm sure she was up to something."

"*Real* detectives don't waste time chasing nutty old ladies," said Otto.

"A real detective...hmmm. That's a good idea. I'll show this purse to Uncle Tooth," said Olivia. "Come on."

"I meant me," said Otto. "*I'm* a real detective!"

But Olivia was too far ahead to hear.

TWO

Uncle Tooth was at home cleaning his pipe. He stopped to listen to Olivia's story.

Otto thought the whole thing was a waste of time. He went into a corner and shot marbles.

When Olivia was finished, Uncle Tooth opened the purse. It was empty, except for a bone comb covered with hair.

"Curious," said Uncle Tooth.

He placed one of the hairs under his microscope.

Suddenly, there was a knock at the door. Otto opened it.

A round little man carrying a briefcase hurried inside.

"This is an emergency!" he cried. "I'm looking for Uncle Tooth, the famous detective!"

"You've found him, by jingo!" replied Uncle Tooth.

"Mr. Tooth, my name is Sedly Mether. I'm afraid I have lost my dear mother's black pearl. I was going to donate it to the Boogle Bay Museum. It was in my briefcase when I boarded the train. But when I got to the museum, the pearl was gone!"

"Was the briefcase ever out of your sight?" asked Uncle Tooth.

Sedly Mether thought for a moment.

"Just once. I went to get a glass of

water for an old lady who was feeling dizzy. I left the briefcase on my seat. When I came back with the water, it was still there. But the old lady was climbing out a window!"

"See?" said Olivia. "I told you she was acting strange."

"I have studied the hair from this comb," said Uncle Tooth. "It is no ordinary hair. It is a cobweb! And that was no ordinary old lady. It was the Cobweb Queen!"

"Who is the Cobweb Queen?" asked Otto.

"An old enemy," said Uncle Tooth. "She makes a game of stealing things. She can always get away because she happens to be a witch!"

"*Wow!* A witch-queen!" cried Olivia. "Does she live in a castle?"

"Yes, in Mookey Swamp," Uncle Tooth went on. "It's my guess she's headed there now. She'll have to go by boat. If we hurry down to the docks, we might catch her!"

Sedly Mether said, "Mr. Tooth, if you recover my dear mother's pearl, I will pay you a handsome reward."

"Heck! I'll do it for free," said Uncle Tooth. "I have a score to settle with that old witch. She once cheated me out of my lucky compass during a game of Go Fish!"

THREE

Uncle Tooth dashed out the door. Otto dashed after him.

Olivia hurried out, too, before Auntie Hick could stop her.

The docks were a busy place. The Cobweb Queen could be anywhere. Otto and Uncle Tooth split up.

Suddenly, Otto found Olivia at his side.

"What are *you* doing here?" he said.

"You don't think I'm going to miss the chance to see a real witch, do you?" she answered.

"But you'll spoil everything!" Otto said.

"That's the idea, isn't it?" Olivia shot

back. "To spoil the Cobweb Queen's plan. Or have you been asleep?"

She pulled Otto behind some crates and pointed to a parrot and a lady with a wide hat.

"Those two look fishy," Olivia whispered.

"Sure…right," said Otto. "Why don't *you* spy on them? I'm going to search in this direction." He ran off.

As Olivia watched, the parrot and the lady stepped onto a black barge. They went into the cabin and shut the door.

Olivia crept on board. She put her ear to the door.

"Isn't it beautiful, Eddy?" said a crackly voice. "A new jewel for my crown."

"The Cobweb Queen!" gasped Olivia.

She was just going to find Otto and Uncle Tooth when the door opened. Olivia hid behind a potato sack.

The parrot flew out and untied the barge from the pier.

"Gun the engines, Eddy," came the crackly voice from the cabin. "It's time we hightailed it out of here."

FOUR

Otto soon found Uncle Tooth. He told him about Olivia. "Isn't that just like a *girl*!" He laughed.

"Was the parrot wearing an eye patch?" asked Uncle Tooth.

"How did you know?" said Otto.

"That parrot is One-eyed Eddy. He's the Cobweb Queen's partner."

"Then that lady with the hat was…"

"The Cobweb Queen herself!" replied Uncle Tooth. "Hurry!"

They dashed back to the dock. The barge was disappearing down the river.

Otto saw Olivia's scarf, caught on a piling.

"They've got Olivia!" he wailed. "It's all my fault!"

"Don't blame yourself," said Uncle Tooth. "We'll get her back."

Just then, Auntie Hick showed up, all out of breath. "There you two are. Where's Olivia?"

"We think she was just kidnapped by the Cobweb Queen," said Uncle Tooth.

"No...here I am," came a voice.

They all turned to see Olivia climbing out of the water. "I had to make a fast getaway," she explained.

"I feel faint," moaned Auntie Hick.

FIVE

They went back to Uncle Tooth's house. Auntie Hick lay down on the sofa to rest her nerves. Soon she was sound asleep.

Olivia dried herself before the fire.

Otto was happy to change out of his new suit. He put on a sweatshirt, set his marbles on the table, and stuck his slingshot into his pocket.

Uncle Tooth got his wooden sword.

"Where's my weapon?" asked Olivia.

"You don't need one," Uncle Tooth told her. "You are staying here with Auntie Hick."

Olivia stamped her foot. "That's not fair! This is *my* case. I was just about to crack it."

"There's too much danger involved for a girl," Otto said as he walked out the door. "Better let a *real* detective handle it."

Olivia watched them head off. "We'll see about that!" she said.

Otto and Uncle Tooth made their way through the dismal swamp until they came to the Cobweb Queen's castle. It sat on its own little island. Her black barge was moored outside.

"We must be very careful," Uncle Tooth warned. "There's no telling what the Cobweb Queen has up her sleeve."

He led the way across the drawbridge. It was draped with cobwebs. As Otto and Uncle Tooth passed through, the cobwebs seemed to come alive and grab them.

WHACK! WHACK!

Uncle Tooth cut the cobwebs away with his sword.

They stepped through the castle entrance into a dark hallway.

There were things lying on the ground—small, round, dark things.

"Eenie Meanies!" whispered Uncle Tooth.

Otto shuddered.

"You didn't tell me there were going to be monsters," he said.

Uncle Tooth poked an Eenie Meanie with his sword. It didn't move.

"They are the Cobweb Queen's guards," he explained. "But they are sound asleep. We'll have to tiptoe past them."

Then Otto and Uncle Tooth heard voices. They crept over to a doorway and looked inside.

SIX

The Cobweb Queen sat on her throne. She was admiring herself in a mirror. One-eyed Eddy stood before her.

"Doesn't this pearl look perfect in my crown?" she asked.

"Magnificent!" agreed Eddy. "You deserve everything you steal."

The Queen glanced at an open treasure chest filled with loot.

"Don't I, though," she giggled.

Otto and Uncle Tooth burst into the room.

"Why, Tooth," said the Cobweb Queen. "What a disgusting surprise! Don't tell me you're still peeved because I won that dumb compass. I hate sore losers!"

"That pearl doesn't belong to you," Uncle Tooth shouted. "Give it back!"

"Pearl?" asked the Queen. "What pearl?"

"Don't play games," said Uncle Tooth.

"Games?" the Cobweb Queen said. "Now you're talking my language. How about a game of Go Fish? If you win, I'll give you the pearl. If I win, I'll feed you to the Eenie Meanies...deal?"

"No deal," said Uncle Tooth. "You cheat!"

One-eyed Eddy drew a pistol from under his wing and cocked the trigger. "I'm afraid you've got no choice," he said.

The Cobweb Queen took something from her treasure chest and tossed it on a card table. "Here, I'll even throw in your old compass."

"All right," said Uncle Tooth. "I'll play."

"Goody!" cried the Queen. "I'll deal!"

She winked at Eddy. "Show the little runt around the castle."

"Righto," said Eddy.

He led Otto out of the throne room and down some stairs. "It's the dungeon for you, my friend," said Eddy. "Your uncle is sure to lose. Then you'll both be lunch for the Eenie Meanies."

He opened a door to a damp, dirty cell. "In you go, matey."

"In *there*?" gasped Otto. "You must be joking!"

"Do I look like the joking sort?" said Eddy. "Get in, or I'll push you in!"

But suddenly, someone pushed *him*!

Eddy tumbled forward into the cell. That same someone slammed the door shut behind him.

It was Olivia!

"What are *you* doing here?" said Otto.

"Saving your skin, for starters," Olivia replied.

"You followed us?" said Otto. "But you're supposed to be with Auntie Hick."

"Oh, stop fussing. She was sound asleep. Besides, I left her a note."

"Well, that should make her feel *much* better," said Otto.

Olivia kicked Eddy's pistol into a corner and started up the stairs. "You can stay here and argue with yourself," she told Otto. "I'm going to get the pearl back."

"Wait up!" Otto called. "I'll come with you."

They searched until they found a stairway to a balcony above the throne room.

From the balcony they could see Uncle Tooth and the Cobweb Queen playing cards.

They watched as Uncle Tooth jumped to his feet. "I win! I win!" he shouted.

"But that's impossible!" cried the Queen.

Uncle Tooth grabbed his lucky compass. "Now, hand over the pearl. A deal's a deal."

"You fool!" hissed the Queen. "I never give anything back!"

"This time, *you've* got no choice!" called Otto.

SEVEN

Otto fitted a stone into his slingshot, took careful aim, and...PING! He knocked the pearl from the Cobweb Queen's crown.

It flew into the air and landed in Uncle Tooth's hands.

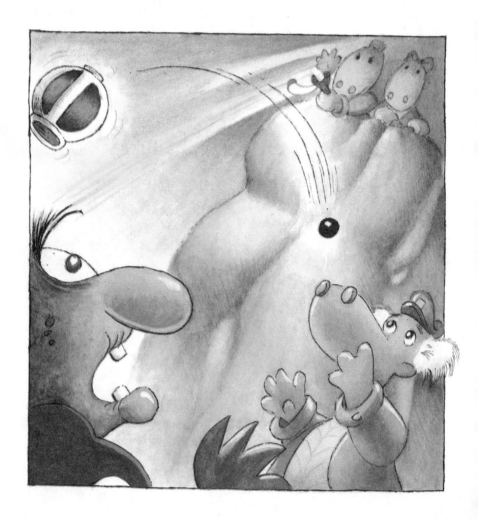

"That's cheating!" she screeched.

"You can't cheat a cheater," said Uncle Tooth.

The Cobweb Queen's eyes glowed bright red, and her hair stood on end.

"We'd better get out of here," said Otto.

He and Olivia ran down the stairs. Uncle Tooth met them in the hall.

The Cobweb Queen came after them. "Guards!" she screamed.

Instantly, the Eenie Meanies woke up. They ran around in circles, bumping into one another.

"After them, you fools!" the Queen
ordered.

The Eenie Meanies chased Otto,
Uncle Tooth, and Olivia down the hall and
out onto the drawbridge.

"Into the barge!" cried Uncle Tooth.

The three of them hopped on board. Uncle Tooth tossed the pearl to Olivia. He tried to hold off the Eenie Meanies with his sword. Otto fired his slingshot over and over. But there were too many Meanies.

In no time, the Eenie Meanies had trapped them on the roof of the cabin.

"Having trouble?" sneered the queen. "Good! I hate sore losers."

"You said that already," said Otto.

"Now, give me the pearl like good sports, or I may have to do something nasty," she said.

"If we do, will you let us go?" asked Olivia.

"Scout's honor," said the Queen.

"No! Don't! She's lying!" cried Otto.

It was too late. Olivia flung the pearl
at the Cobweb Queen, who grabbed for it,
and missed. The pearl hit the drawbridge,
bounced three times, and rolled over the
edge.

"My pearl!" wailed the Queen. She got
down on her hands and knees and peered
into the swamp. "You idiot! You lost my
pearl!"

All the Eenie Meanies jumped off the

barge and went over to the drawbridge
to look.

Uncle Tooth gunned the engine. The
barge sped into the swamp.

"I'll get you for this, Tooth," the
Cobweb Queen screeched after them. "I'll
get you if it's the last thing I ever do!"

In a flash, they left the Cobweb
Queen's castle far behind.

EIGHT

"I'm glad I got my compass back," said Uncle Tooth. "But I guess it isn't so lucky after all. We lost Sedly Mether's pearl."

"How could you *do* that?" Otto said to Olivia. "Throwing that pearl was *so* dumb!"

"Relax," said Olivia. "The pearl is right here."

She reached into her pocket and handed the black pearl to Uncle Tooth.

"See! Your compass *is* lucky," she said.

Otto was confused.

"But I saw you throw the pearl at the Cobweb Queen."

"That wasn't the pearl. It was one of your marbles," Olivia explained. "I thought it might come in handy."

"You took my marble without asking?" said Otto.

"I had to," answered Olivia. "Besides, it worked, didn't it?"

"Well...yes," Otto admitted. "I only wish *I'd* thought of it."

Uncle Tooth laughed. "If that doesn't beat all! Olivia, you have the makings of..."

"A *real* detective!" said Otto.

Olivia smiled. "Thanks," she said.